To my son Jamie—M.T.

First published in the United States 1999 by
LITTLE TIGER PRESS
N16 W23390 Stoneridge Drive, Waukesha, WI 53188
Originally published in Great Britain 1998 by
Bloomsbury Publishing Plc
Text copyright © Faustin Charles
Illustrations copyright © Michael Terry
All rights reserved
CIP Data is available
ISBN 1-888444-56-8
Printed in Belgium by Proost NV, Turnhout
First American Edition
1 3 5 7 9 10 8 6 4 2

THE SELFISH CROCODILE

Faustin Charles and Michael Terry

Little Tiger Press

In a river deep in the forest, there lived a large crocodile. He was a very selfish crocodile. He didn't want any other creature to drink or bathe in the river. He thought it was HIS river.

Every day he shouted to the creatures of the forest, "Stay away from the river! It's MY river! And if you come into my river, I'll eat you up!"

So there were no fish, no tadpoles, no frogs, no crabs, no crayfish in the river. They were all afraid of the selfish crocodile.

The forest creatures kept away from the river, too. Whenever they were thirsty, they had to go for miles out of their way to drink in other rivers and streams.

Every day the crocodile lay in the sun on his great big back, picking his big sharp teeth with a stick.

Early one morning the forest animals were awakened by a loud groaning sound. Something was in terrible pain.

The creatures thought it must be an animal caught by the crocodile.

GROAN

But as the bright sun came out, they saw that it was the crocodile himself who was in pain. He was lying on his big back, holding his swollen jaw, and crying real tears.

GROAN

The creatures drew closer—but not too close. Some of them felt sorry for the crocodile.

"What's the matter with him?" asked a deer.

"I don't know," said a squirrel.

"Maybe he's going to die," chirped a blackbird.

"If that happens, it'll be safe to go into the river again!" grunted a wild pig.

The animals thought about it. They hung from branches, they peeked through the grass, they buzzed in the air. They shook their heads as they watched the great big crocodile. But no one tried to help.

Suddenly, a little mouse appeared, sniffing the air.
He ran along the crocodile's tail, then onto his stomach.
The other creatures stared.

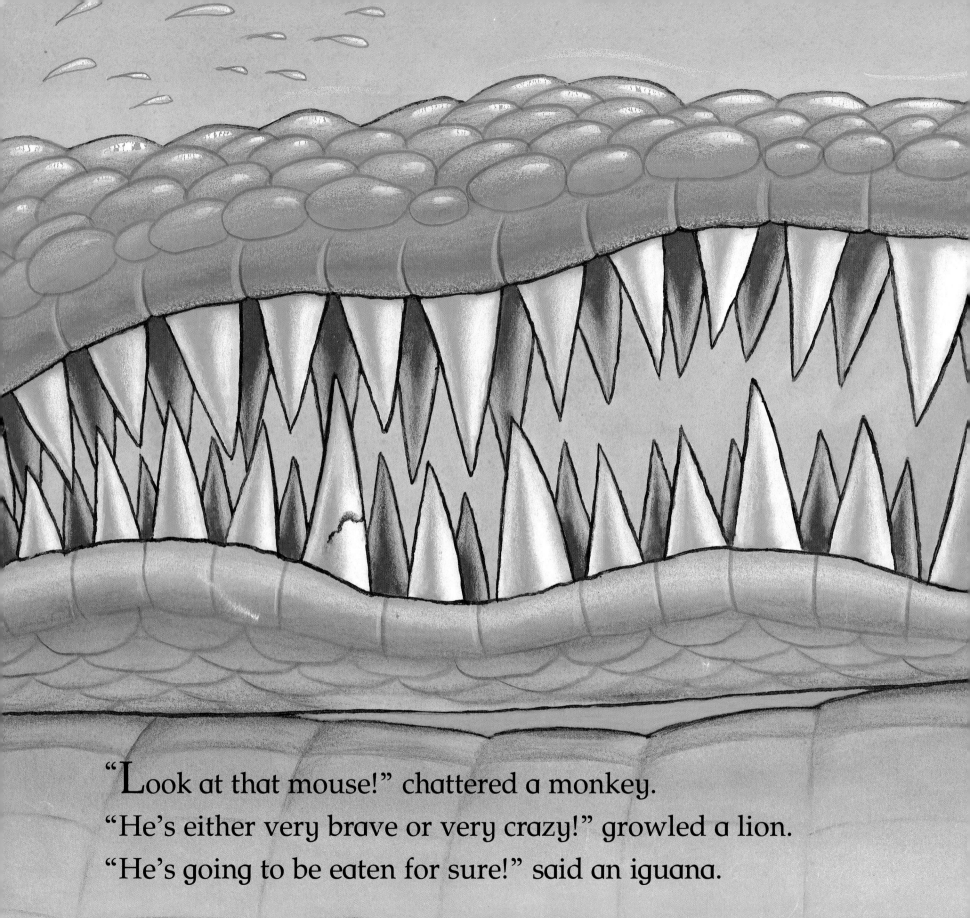

"Look at that mouse!" chattered a monkey.

"He's either very brave or very crazy!" growled a lion.

"He's going to be eaten for sure!" said an iguana.

The mouse crept along the crocodile's big neck and
into his open mouth.

There was a hush in the forest.

The mouse took hold of something and pulled and pulled and pulled. Finally, he pulled it out, put it on his shoulder, and walked out of the crocodile's mouth.

The astonished creatures began to cheer.

The crocodile sat up and said, "The pain is all gone!"
Then he saw the mouse walking down his stomach, carrying
an enormous crocodile tooth on his shoulder.

"Your bad tooth was giving you a toothache!" said the mouse, turning around to face the now smiling crocodile. "Do you want it back?"

"On no, no, no, get rid of it, and when you're finished,

come back. I have a present for you."

The mouse buried the bad tooth under a tree, and when he
returned, the crocodile had a nice, juicy nut waiting for him.

As the crocodile watched the mouse eat his nut, he said, "You must be very smart if you can cure a toothache—and very kind, too. I'm so grateful. But what should I do if my toothache comes back?"

"Don't worry, I'll help you take care of your teeth," answered the mouse, nibbling.

Soon the crocodile and the mouse were best friends.

Not long after, the crocodile sent all the animals an invitation. "Please come to drink and bathe in the river! I won't hurt you! The river belongs to all of us!" he said.

The creatures weren't afraid to drink and bathe in the river anymore. Although the crocodile was sometimes a little grumpy, they grew to love him.

And soon the river was once again full of fish and tadpoles and frogs and crabs and crayfish.